For my parents

Red Fox Books are published by Random House Children's Books, 61–63 Uxbridge Road, London W5 5SA, a division of THE RANDOM HOUSE GROUP LTD, in Australia by RANDOM HOUSE AUSTRALIA (PTY) LTD, 20 Alfred Street, Milsons Point, Sydney, NSW 2061, Australia in New Zealand by RANDOM HOUSE NEW ZEALAND LTD, 18 Poland Road, Glenfield, Auckland 10, New Zealand In South Africa by RANDOM HOUSE (PTY) LTD, Endulini, 5A Jubilee Road, Parktown 2193, South Africa THE RANDOM HOUSE GROUP Limited Reg. No. 954009 www.kidsatrandomhouse.co.uk

The Bodley Head edition published 2004 Red Fox edition published 2005 Copyright © Caroline Glicksman, 2004

ERIC AND THE RED PLANET A RED FOX BOOK 0 009 45640 6 First published

illustrator of this work has been asserted in accordance with the Copyright, Designs and Patents Act, 1988.

an imprint of Random House Children's Books

10 9 8 7 6 5 4 3 2 1

Printed and bound in China

A CIP catalogue record for this book is available from the British Library.

The right of Caroline Glicksman and illustrator of this work

of Random House Children's Books

Eric and the Red Planet

Caroline Glicksman

RED FOX

Eric is a very unusual bear. He's red and he's very, very clever, especially with numbers.

He loves numbers as much as he loves honey.

So put honey and numbers together and you get Eric's dream breakfast – a bowl of Honey Number Puffs.

... an histori[c] day ...

HONEY NUMBER PUFFS™

THE GROWLER

MARS LIFT-OFF TODAY

PROBABILITY IN PRACTICE

GROWLER TRAVEL

HONEY

It said:

CONGRATULATIONS!
You are eating the millionth box of **HONEY NUMBER PUFFS™!** Bring a friend to the SpaceBear Space Base and enjoy a day in a million!

For the first time ever, Eric didn't add up his breakfast. He didn't even eat it!

Instead he rushed to the phone . . .

. . . and ten minutes later, he was scooting out of town with his best friend Erica, the only bear he has ever met who loves numbers as much as he does.

The space base was very exciting. Eric and Erica were given their very own space suits and shown around by a very important bear. They saw:

TEN computers in mission control

NINE posters of different planets

EIGHT astronauts training

SEVEN busy robot bears

SIX saws in the rocket workshop

The most exciting part of Eric's prize was a visit to the fastest rocket ever built.

MARS EXPRESS

Its fuel tank had just been filled up with ten huge jars of honey, ready to go to Mars!

Eric and Erica were allowed to go right inside the rocket.

SPACE HELMETS

SPACE BISCUITS

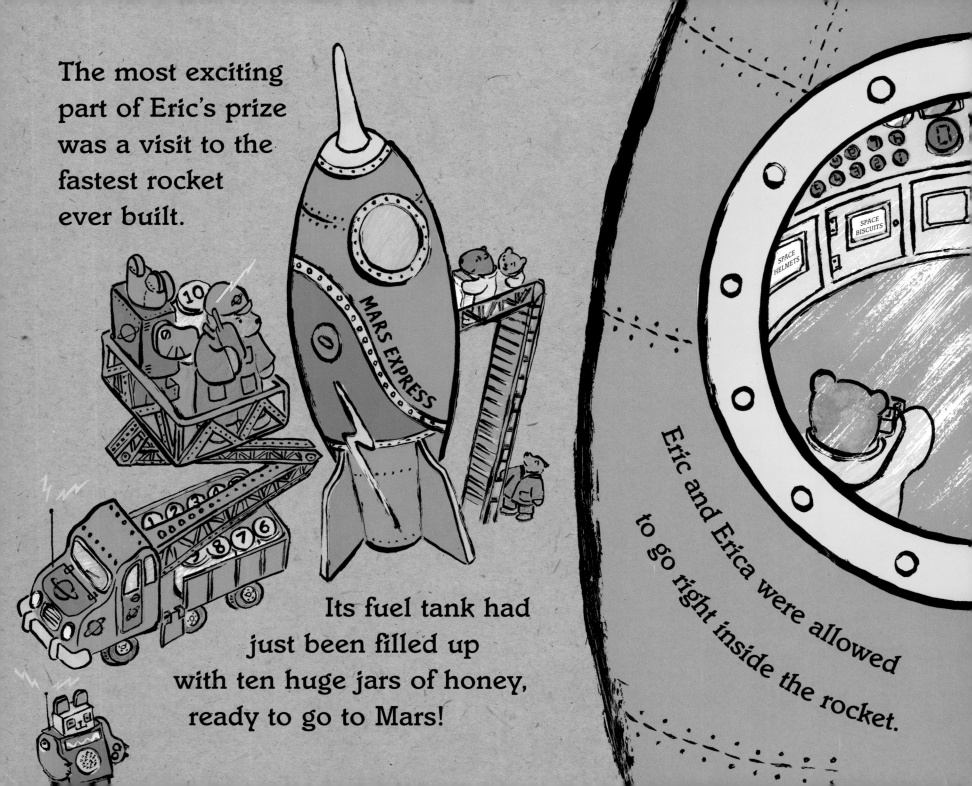

Erica took lots of photos and Eric glowed very red.

Eric couldn't resist pressing some of the bright-red flashing numbers . . .

. . . just like a real astronaut counting down to . . .

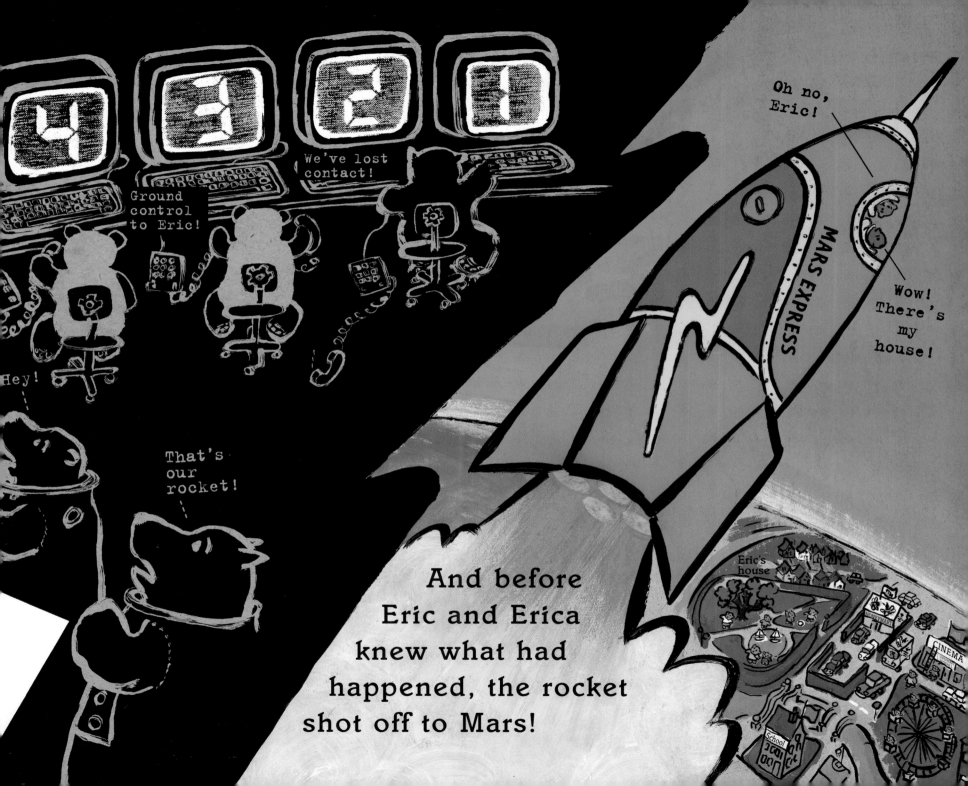

Eric and Erica soon got the hang of floating around the cabin.

IN EMERGENCY CUT HOLE

WATER

FUEL

Much better than boring space biscuits!

Asteroid Belt

Mars

Earth

SpaceBear Universal Space Map no.19

HONEY NUMBER PUFFS™

SPACE-O-METER

SPACE BISCUITS

Before long they were hungry. Luckily, Erica found ten huge jars of honey in a cupboard.

Erica ate two whole jars . . .

. . . and Eric ate three.

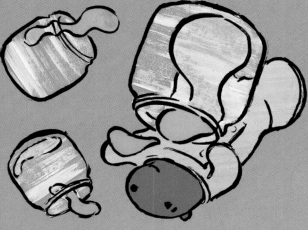

(Well, it's a long way to Mars.)

As soon as they landed on Mars, Eric and Erica climbed out of the rocket. They were the first bears ever to set foot on the red planet.

EXIT

LADDER

HAVE YOU REMEMBERED YOUR HELMET?

AIR

It's not as red as I expected.

Erica took lots more photos.
Eric collected lots of rocks.

But it was very cold and Earth
looked a long way away.
Suddenly they felt lonely.
It was time to go home.

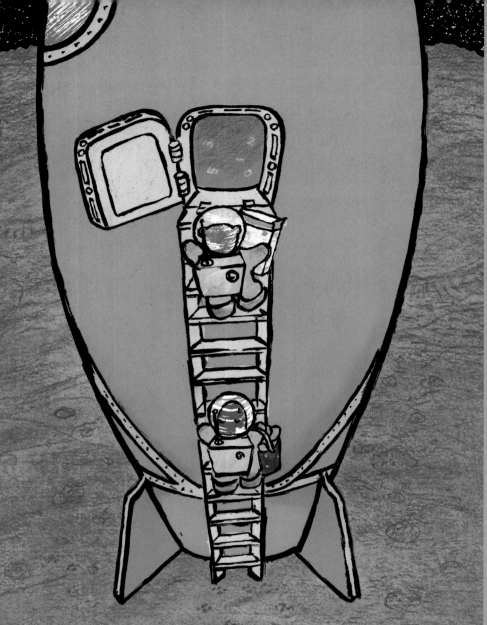

They climbed back into the rocket. It was much warmer inside.

"Ten seconds to lift off!" said Eric. He counted down just as before, pressing each button in turn.

Nothing happened.
Eric couldn't understand
what was wrong.
He was sure he hadn't
made a mistake with
his counting.
Suddenly Erica
grabbed his paw.

"Look!" she gasped. "The fuel tank! It's empty! We're stuck on Mars!"

Eric thought very hard.

The rocket had used ten jars of honey to fly to Mars so . . .

. . . it must need another ten to fly home.

"The honey . . . " he said, as he ran to look in the cupboard.

I ate three jars . . . . . . and I ate two.

HONEY NUMBER PUFFS

TO REFILL THE FUEL TANK

There were only five jars left. "Well, it's no use getting halfway home," said Erica. She licked her paw thoughtfully.

Then suddenly Erica started
jumping round the cabin.
"Eric!" she shouted.
"The dust on
my paws!
It's sweet!

THERE'S
HONEY
ON
MARS!"

Eric looked at the rocks he'd collected. They were melting. He gave one of them a careful lick. It was honey!

Luckily there was a saw for use in an emergency.

IN EMERGENCY CUT HOLE

SPACE MAPS

Once the tank's full, let's fill up all ten jars again. Then we can eat six on the way home...

Eric and Erica climbed back outside. They sawed a hole through the frozen rock. There was warm, gooey honey underneath!

... and we'll have four jars for our getting home party!

They filled up the five empty jars with honey. Now they had ten full jars, enough to fill the tank right up. Everything was very sticky and Eric glowed very red!

At last, they climbed back into the rocket. Eric took a deep breath and counted down once again ...

Phew! With a huge roar the rocket shot back towards Earth.

Eric and Erica floated happily around the cabin. "Well, I'm glad we didn't end up stuck on Mars," said Erica.

"I know," said Eric, licking a sticky Martian rock, "but imagine living on a planet made of honey!"

Erica smiled.
"Perhaps someone does," she said.

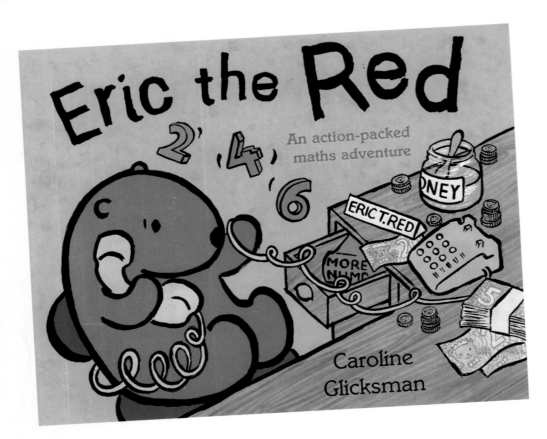